蔡榮勇 著
Poems by Tsai Jung-yung

戴珍妮 譯
Translated by Jane Deasy

念念
詩穎

Continuous
Thoughts of Sherrie

蔡榮勇漢英雙語詩集
Chinese – English

台灣詩叢 • Taiwan Poetry Series 06

唯一的真實
是永不褪色的悲哀

——葉笛〈輓歌——悼亡兄〉

The only truth
Is never-fading grief

——Ye Di "An Elegy: Mourning My Late Brother"

【總序】詩推台灣意象

叢書策劃／李魁賢

　　進入21世紀，台灣詩人更積極走向國際，個人竭盡所能，在詩人朋友熱烈參與支持下，策畫出席過印度、蒙古、古巴、智利、緬甸、孟加拉、馬其頓等國舉辦的國際詩歌節，並編輯《台灣心聲》等多種詩選在各國發行，使台灣詩人心聲透過作品傳佈國際間。接續而來的國際詩歌節邀請愈來愈多，已經有應接不暇的趨向。

　　多年來進行國際詩交流活動最困擾的問題，莫如臨時編輯帶往國外交流的選集，大都應急處理，不但時間緊迫，且選用作品難免會有不週。因此，興起策畫【台灣詩叢】雙語詩系的念頭。若台灣詩人平常就有雙語詩集出版，隨時可以應用，詩作交流與詩人交誼雙管齊下，更具實際成效，對台灣詩的國際交流活動，當更加順利。

　　以【台灣】為名，著眼點當然有鑑於台灣文學在國際間名目不彰，台灣詩人能夠有機會在國際努力開拓空間，非為個人建立知名度，而是為推展台灣意象的整體事功，期待開創台灣文學的長久景象，才能奠定寶貴的歷史意義，台灣文學終必在世界文壇上佔有地位。

　　實際經驗也明顯印證，台灣詩人參與國際詩交流活動，很受重視，帶出去的詩選集也深受歡迎，從近年外國詩人和出版社與本人合作編譯台灣詩選，甚至主動翻譯本人詩集在各國文學雜誌或詩刊發表，進而出版外譯詩集的情況，大為增多，即可充分證明。

　　承蒙秀威資訊科技公司一本支援詩集出版初衷，慨然接受【台灣詩叢】列入編輯計畫，對台灣詩的國際交流，提供推進力量，希望能有更多各種不同外語的雙語詩集出版，形成進軍國際的集結基地。

2017.02.15誌

序詩

不知不覺
七月的陽光呼喚著
阿勃勒的黃金花朵

詩穎和大大攝影夥伴
在樹下拍照
初夏，不肯炎熱

試著　摘下
阿勃勒的小黃花
念念書寫著悲慟

我想像著詩穎在天堂
渴望跟林老師和這群好朋友
一同談笑照相

阿勃勒繼續想念
阿勃勒繼續開花
我想像著詩穎手持照相機

附記：2012年6月6日詩穎在中榮住院，「大大攝影」林錫銘老師、阿俊、
　　　玉娟、和郭妹妹，詩穎帶著新買的鏡頭，和大夥在國美館阿勃勒樹
　　　下拍照。郭妹妹還帶來一隻青蛙，讓詩穎拍照，讓她過了一個快樂
　　　的初夏。

目次

五月二十四日

五月二十四日
那一天
一張X光片
一通長途電話
晨曦　網住
癌症散落的身影

窗外黃脈刺桐
層層疊疊的綠葉子
包裹著詩穎的癌細胞

詩穎　我的心肝寶貝
肺部的癌細胞　阿爹搆不著
好像遠在英國留學的你

青春剛剛冒出的花苞
死神卻把螢火蟲似的癌細胞
放入肺部裡繁殖

這個玩笑
甜蜜的家庭　921大地震
找不到逃生的出口

心情不知要如何　放慢
歲月的腳步　找尋
生命細微的光　緩慢

附記：詩穎咳嗽咳個不停，可能得肺結核，2012年5月24日，到台
　　　北市衛生局檢查，醫生判斷是肺癌。

輓歌

我的心肝寶貝　詩穎
墜落地上　翡翠的青春
留下滿地　綺麗的回憶

山上的百合花　尚未吐出花苞
二月的春風　銜哀嘆了一口氣
她是一株有氣質的百合花

到英國新堡大學
找尋波特筆下的兔子
追尋草原上跳躍的蹤影

扛著超大行旅箱的　夢想
躲在統聯遊覽車　道再見
坐飛機到英國追　夢想

扛著超大行旅箱的　理想
站在村宇大門口
按電鈴　**我回家了**

一張X光片
誤落癌網中
一去八個多月

肺部的癌細胞大量繁殖流竄
生命掉漆龜裂
難以遏止　難以停歇

二月十七日　深夜
一再努力的想　坐起來
一再努力的想⋯⋯呼吸

二月十八日　凌晨五點
床鋪搖撼的晃動
噴泉湧流的小地震

早晨七點二十分
天空烏雲密布　太陽破雲而出
一朵勇敢且潔白的百合花

脈管裡住滿耶穌滿滿的愛
不是血液
永遠的安息在宇宙

附記：2013年早晨在中榮醫院病逝。春天仍然救不了她。以為過了
　　　春天生命或許會吐新芽。

給遠方的詩穎

立榮大鳥
藍天白雲的天空
找不到**遠**方

台中與金門相離400公里
短針移動一小格　剛喝完一杯綠茶
遠方　降落了

詩穎的癌細胞　蛀壞了
歲月的坑道　背起Sherrie的青春
穿越長長且漆黑的坑道

詩穎　就是遠方
立榮大鳥降落金門尚義機場
卻無法降落　詩穎的靈

阿爹　背著你的好朋友相機
詩穎　你到達機場了嗎
跟著一起拍照吧

詩篇

背著　詩穎的照相機
喀嚓　讚美你的善良
喀嚓　榮耀你的勇敢

藍天白雲　晴天空
詩穎的肺　出頭天
走在坑道　上天堂

風獅爺　請你告訴我
東北風的　哀愁
要如何鎮壓

記憶的記憶　淡水
對著建功嶼　拍照
書寫哀愁的　氛圍

．

她在天堂
我在金門
落日的哀愁

打開鏡頭　海浪告知
詩穎在岸上揮手
鏡頭對不到焦距

詩穎就是圓點

圓點就是一切
詩穎
是圓點的一切

生命一個點
一萬粒子中的一點
度量宇宙的無限
詩穎圓點凋謝了嗎

天文數字的斑點
編織巨大且虛無的蜘蛛
網住，自我的消融
他者的圓點和宇宙的無限

一切就是圓點的無限
圓點詩穎，一切無限

附記：詩中有些句子抄自《草間彌生自傳》44至45頁。木馬出版社。
　　　女兒上天堂後，思念的圓點布滿全身，甚至她的遺物也布滿
　　　圓點。

幾公分

生和死
只是時間征服了時間

——葉笛

用尺測量
詩穎的一生
會是幾公分的風景

測量
出生、死亡的尺
看得見刻度嗎

我哭泣

夜深了　躺下來
伸一伸　手　腳
彎一彎　手　腳
眼睛試著打開夢的窗戶

詩穎的肺腺癌
包圍著肺　靜坐抗議

翻過來　碰牆
翻過去　撞牆
我哭泣只能我哭泣
眼睛默默的記憶著愛

一點也不冷

詩穎
躺在冷凍庫
冰冷吧

不要害怕
阿爹阿母和姐姐愛你的心
守護在你身邊　不要哭泣

找不到衣服穿
記得把我們的愛
趕緊穿在身上　不要覷腆

阿爹，您不用擔憂
您和阿母姐姐對我的愛
我穿在身上　一點也不冷

阿爹，我愛你

我在天堂已經住了一年
日子過得很春天

外婆、外公、阿公對我很好
時常聚在一起吃飯聊天

我，有空也繼續拍照
阿爹，相機不要再掉下去

想念家人時，偷偷的飛到人間
偷窺妳們過得如何，ㄎㄎ　ㄎㄎ……

阿爹，不用擔心
我不會再偏食了

阿爹，不要悲傷
我的手機收聽得到喔

您不要再想念我了

阿爹

您不要再想念　流淚

對不起

我不能讓您牽著我的手

走過地毯的那一端

也許生一堆孩子

不管是男孩或女孩

就像外公牽著我和姐姐去上學

您不要再想念我了

阿爹，我在天堂

不會偏食了

也會養成運動的好習慣

也會繼續拍照繼續旅行

也會……

也會思念流淚

之前與之後

死亡以癌症出現也不足怪
只因世上「生」太孤單

——葉笛

生病之前
一切都是希望
一切都是夢想
坐下來聊天，風也會惡作劇

生病之後
向上帝禱告
向佛祖求救
向天公求救
向醫生求救
向死神求救
向夢祈求盼望
向詩懇求奇蹟

向朝陽購買時間
向食物乞求活下去
向明天跪下來祈禱
向自己的意志挑戰

死亡之後
大海一切歸零
聽不見波浪退潮的說話聲

飛走的麻雀

活下去的理由
愈來愈少

閱讀，那麼多文學家的作品
閱讀，那麼多哲學家的思想
閱讀，那麼多藝術家的畫作
仍然，找不到希望的燈
黑暗老是告訴我，放棄吧

看見一隻麻雀，孤單駐留枝頭上
跳上跳下　望了又望
箭，一般的飛向遠方

活下的理由
愈來愈模糊

詩穎像枝頭上的麻雀
箭，一般的飛向遠方

閱讀佛經，佛陀，也是一隻飛走的麻雀
閱讀聖經，耶穌，也是一隻飛走的麻雀
還是找不到可以棲息的樹枝

清明節

我們相約　在主裡
共同生活　常相憶
我們相約　在主裡
將來有一天要　再歡聚

驟然，一聲巨響
嘔出，悲
吐出，傷

回憶過去日子裡
縱有歡笑，也有淚滴
捨不得告訴你
在主的愛裡　我等著你

日子，伸出雙手
試著，打包
詩穎的青春

在主裡祝福你
我在主裡思念你
願主帶領你
進入迦南地

我們相約　不　遠
就是，呼吸不到
她的青春

我們相約　在主裡
聽見，斑鳩在屋頂上
咕嚕　咕嚕嚕
天　　亮了

幽蘭露

一如
火車站的置物櫃
放入一個小甕

裝入二十九歲的青春年華
無草茵　相陪
無松蓋　陪伴

太陽發高燒
無風扇　吹
無冷氣　涼

哭不出聲音的詩穎
夜黑黑的，閱讀
李賀的詩〈蘇小小墓〉

鬼門關開了
記得回家
吃摩斯漢堡

淡水車站

立榮　孤鳥
從金門尚義機場
飛往　台北松山機場
（阿爹完成了詩穎金門之旅）

住在水調歌頌民宿
吃過晚餐　阿爹和林老師
共飲金門58高粱　共話
詩穎學習攝影的熱情

早上起床　大夥　背著相機
搶拍　戴勝的生活起居
阿爹老是按不下快門
光線　喜歡躲在暗處
小聲呼喚你的小名　阿穎

大夥　喀嚓的　喀嚓的　此起彼落
（物象無法還原真相）
快門是阿爹的心情
ISO是肺腺癌的細胞繁殖
光圈是詩穎的青春

一不小心，思念
標準鏡頭　滾地　呼應
相機墜地　呼應　思念

（詩穎一定會說：「臭阿爹！笨手笨腳！」）

坐在飛機上
窗外　漂浮著朵朵雪白的雲絮
隱隱約約現出　你甜美的笑容

立榮　孤鳥
降落在松山機場
走出金門的歲月坑道
坐上捷運　找尋詩穎的包包
醒目的「**淡水線**」
就像一把水果刀
為一粒蘋果削皮
正在剝落　孤單
Life少了一點家人的慰藉

坐在高鐵列車
心情高速的哀傷
列印著詩穎的病痛史

請問列車長
有沒有　詩穎的車班

我的老

詩穎，29歲
還未老
人生就結束
留下，我的老
數數　念念

傳說

百合花，是這樣凋謝的
肺癌佔據了，詩穎的肺

百合花，是這樣凋謝的
詩穎，掙脫死神的懷抱

百合花，是這樣凋謝的
詩穎，帶不走自己的相機

百合花，是這樣凋謝的
詩穎，留下星星的閃爍

百合花謝了，明年還會再盛開
詩穎，凋謝了　永遠　凋謝了

上帝，繼續讓人禱告
佛陀，繼續讓人膜拜

詩穎，留下人間一則傳說
地球則繼續寫傳說

也許吧

> 我們腳底下沉重的地球
> 不會飄然消失，永遠不會
>
> ——茨維嗒耶娃

消失在人間的詩穎
地球，感受不到
一片飄落的嫩葉

有一天
我也在人間消失
不知誰還會，繼續
思念，她溫柔的名字

姐姐及她的孩子
也許吧
再來會是誰……

一輩子

詩穎還來不及

追憶　阿爹

卻要　讓阿爹傷慟

思念你　一輩子

擦拭

憂傷的眼眸
難以擦拭
難以擦拭的
詩穎的肺腺癌

哭泣的眼神
難以擦拭
難以擦拭的
詩穎的肺腺癌

夢中的眼眸
難以擦拭
難以擦拭的
詩穎的肺腺癌

破曉的眼眸
難以擦拭

難以擦拭的
詩穎的肺腺癌

死亡的眼眸
或許可以擦拭
詩穎的肺腺癌
一切歸零

上天堂的前一刻

心臟奮力的掙脫
死神的黑手

床鋪　搖晃
死神的黑手

醫生躲在角落
嘆氣

詩穎的呼吸聲
驚醒了地球
喚醒了天堂

栗喉蜂虎

振翅做父親的責任
勇於飛翔的冒險
咬住了一隻蜜蜂　肥滋滋的
飛入窩裡釋放父親的慈愛
翅膀鼓動著　喜悅的聲響
餵食　小寶貝

晚餐後　在月光下振翅高飛
獵捕美味可口的昆蟲

栗喉蜂虎　頂著大太陽
表演高空特技　誘捕蜜蜂

坐在樹蔭下　伸出長鏡頭
找尋詩穎的蹤影
阿爹也是隻迷途的栗喉蜂虎
找不到藍天白雲的　天空

詩穎　你知道嗎
阿爹也是一隻栗喉蜂虎

Sherrie對不起

阿爹不是上帝　解救你　不能
阿爹不是佛祖　拯救你　不能
阿爹不是媽祖　保佑你　不能
阿爹不是醫生　治療你　不能

阿爹僅僅是阿爹……

阿爹僅僅會哭泣
阿爹僅僅會盼望
阿爹很想替你痛苦
無奈
阿爹還是偷偷哭泣

詩穎　你上天堂了
阿爹仍然哭泣……

孔雀魚

蚊帳圍起來的床
蚊子鑽進肺　和癌細胞
一同攻擊　肺氣泡

凌晨　詩穎的咳嗽聲
鬧鐘般的準時　　響起
妻和我不約而同　站在
她身旁驅趕　　死神

活著竟然是　　煎烤
詩穎漆黑的　　未來
童年頑皮的模樣　襲來

「阿爹，你要為我找一位神經內科醫師」
「阿爹，我害怕變成阿呆！」
「阿爹，快來救我！……」

醒來，我只是一尾
困在水族箱的孔雀魚

甜美的嫩葉

詩穎甜美的嫩葉
阿爹層層疊疊的覆葉
呼喚　樹根的親情

一直認為你很獨立
直到你生病了
打開放心的窗戶
你不懂照顧自己的身體
你不會照顧自己的身體

阿爹來不及　對你說
我愛你
一如早凋的玫瑰花
花瓣　來不及美麗
甚至刺痛

X光，照不出

X光，照不出
自我的絕望
關於虛幻的永恆　鐫刻
在烏龜的硬殼

不捨晝夜流逝的時光
永恆被病痛醃漬
青春找不到出口
千里馬　吶喊　馳騁

詩穎癌細胞始於何處
找不到棲息的地方
或許只是一群野獸
衝破肺的柵欄

肺的夜空　布滿
艾瑞莎　德舒緩　歐洲紫三醇……

始終找不到　繁星
癌細胞掩蓋了夜空

X光，照不出
神的光環
神來自何方
來自禱告的聲音嗎

絕望的自我
陽光照得進來嗎
今日就是永恆
一朵野百合在心底　搖曳

拜訪肺葉

我敲了敲　肺葉的前門
「我是詩穎的爸爸
　請你讓我進去
　我想跟癌細胞小天使聊天」

「走開！」
肺葉生氣的說

「他們正在打仗
　小天使變臉
　不斷侵占白血球的國土
　戰事激烈
　你不能進來！」

我敲了敲　肺葉的前門
「我是詩穎的爸爸
　請你讓我進去

我想要當白血球的和平大使
說服小天使」

肺葉冷冷的說
「詩穎才能說服小天使」

「小天使只聽從
　詩穎的信心與毅力
　做為父親的你
　禱告吧！」

我敲了敲　肺葉的前門
「我是詩穎的爸爸
　請你讓我進去
　我的心情一定要進去」

「詩穎的肺葉
　不認識詩穎的爸爸
　甚至不認識詩穎」

肺葉淡定的說
「沒有門呀！」

黑眼睛

一直沒有勇氣睜開
黑夜送給我的黑眼睛
細心找尋相片裡
詩穎的青春年華

有一道光，穿過
菩提樹，活著的
明鏡台，到處照亮
傷痛，慧能您錯了
何處有明鏡台，奈何
奈何明鏡潔淨不了

2016年，今天知道
如何**翻轉**　明天
明天是菩提樹

每一片葉子
都是明鏡台

然而2006年
她在英國Newcastle大學
追夢
還沒看見明鏡台
菩提樹就鬼乾了

黑夜送給我的黑眼睛
找不到
日子失去的光
夢，碎了一地的玻璃
不能再盛水，插一朵紅玫瑰吧！
一首詩，像一塊朱紅的豬肉
吊在天空中
叫喊著

忘掉吧
死蔭幽谷的我

直起腰來，梅花又開了

名字

走進百貨公司
我呼叫她的名字
每一位年輕女孩
躲藏著她的名字
在遠方的天堂思念的記憶
我不可能忘掉你的名字

打開相機拍照
老是有一個背影
手持相機眼睛，凝視著觀景窗
喀嚓一聲　分不清楚是她還是我
我不可能忘掉你的名字

走進你的房間
打開抽屜
打開衣櫥

翻閱書櫃的書籍
啊！名字沾滿灰塵

後記：人因為有悲傷，歡樂往往在身邊溜走，沉浸在悲傷的時光
　　　中，鏡子是失明的，回憶好像有翅膀。寫完這幾首詩後，我
　　　不懂得珍惜相處的時光，總以為她會活得比我長久，一時竟
　　　然不知如何悲傷。

卷尾

感謝女兒詩穎讓阿爹發現死亡的真面目！死亡是真實的！

  在庭院的邊緣，
  在檸檬樹的寂靜下，
  死亡溫柔地吟唱。
  以母親般的灼熱唱給
  那正在傾聽的人。

      ——卡柔·布拉橋（Coral Bracho）

        2016.12.27 再修

作者簡介

　　蔡榮勇，1955年出生於台灣彰化縣北斗鎮，台中師專畢業。現為笠詩社社務兼編輯委員、台灣現代詩人協會常務監事、滿天星兒童文學理事、世界詩人組織（PPDM）會員。曾出版詩集《生命的美學》、《洗衣婦》及合集多種。2009年曾赴蒙古參加台蒙詩歌交流，2014年分別參加在古巴及智利舉行的國際詩歌節。

譯者簡介

　　戴珍妮，生於愛爾蘭，長於台灣，現居溫哥華的中英文譯者，並為加拿大卑詩省翻譯者學會準會員，以及加拿大文學翻譯者協會（位於蒙特婁康考迪亞大學）會員。

Continuous

Thoughts of Sherrie

Prologue

Unknowingly
July's sunshine calls out for
The golden flowers of the golden shower tree

Sherrie and her companions from Dada Photography
Take photos under the tree
Early summer, is unwilling to be scorching hot

Try, to pick
A little yellow flower from the golden shower tree
Continuous thoughts write of grief

I imagine Sherrie in heaven
Longing to chat, to laugh, to take photos together with
Teacher Lin and this group of good friends

The golden shower tree continues to miss

The golden shower tree continues to blossom

I imagine Sherrie holding her camera in her hands

Note:On June 6th, 2012, Sherrie was hospitalized in Taichung Veterans
General Hospital. Teacher Ximing Lin, Ajun, Yujuan and Little
Sister Guo from Dada Photography, along with Sherrie and her
newly-purchased camera lens, were together at the National
Taiwan Museum of Fine Arts taking photos under the golden
shower trees. Little Sister Guo even brought a frog along, for
Sherrie to take photos, allowing her to enjoy a happy early
summer.

May 24th

May 24th
That day
A piece of x-ray film
A long distance phone call
At dawn's first light, captured in a net
Cancer's scattered silhouette

The variegated coral tree outside the window
Layers and layers of green leaves
Enfolded Sherrie's cancer cells

Sherrie, my precious darling
The cancer cells in your lungs, Dad couldn't reach them
Like when you were faraway studying abroad in England

念念詩穎
Continuous Thoughts of Sherrie

The newly sprouted flower buds of youth

Yet Death inserted the firefly-like cancer cells

Into the lungs to multiply

This joke

A sweet family, the 921 earthquake

Cannot find an exit to escape

I don't know how to, slow down, my mood

The footsteps of the years, seek

The fine light of life is, slow

Note:Sherrie had been coughing non-stop, perhaps she had tuberculosis.
      Examined at the Taipei City Department of Health on May 24th
      2012, doctors diagnosed her with lung cancer.

An Elegy

My sweetheart Sherrie
Fell to the ground, her emerald youth
Left on the floor, beautiful memories

The lilies upon the mountain, there flower buds have not yet
blossomed
The spring breeze of February, sighs a sorrowful breath
She is an elegant lily flower

To Newcastle University in England
In search of the rabbit beneath Potter's pen
Chasing after the jumping traces of the grasslands

Carrying an oversized luggage of dreams
Hiding on the Ubus coach, saying goodbye
Taking a flight to England to chase, dreams

Carrying an oversized luggage of ideals
Standing by the main entrance to the village
Pressing the doorbell, I'm home

An x-ray film
Mistakenly fell into the web of cancer
Once gone, it was more than eight months

The cancer cells in the lungs multiplied greatly and fled in all
        directions
The paint of life is chipped and cracked
It is hard to hold back, hard to cease

February 17th, in the depth of the night
She again and again wanted to sit up
She again and again wanted to...breathe

February 18th, five o'clock in the morning

The bed, rocked and shook

A small earthquake with a surging fountain

At twenty past seven in the morning

Dark clouds gathered in the sky, the sun broke out through the
    clouds

A brave and pure white lily

Blood vessels are full to the brim with the love of Jesus

Not blood

Forever resting peacefully in the universe

Note:She died from an illness in Taichung Veterans General Hospital on
    a morning in 2013. Spring, as before, could not save her. I thought
    that perhaps after passing through Spring, shoots of new life could
    spring out.

To Sherrie, Far Away

UNI Air's grand birds
Blue sky, white clouds
Cannot find, a distant place

Taichung and Kinmen are separated by 400 kilometres
The short hand moves one little section, just after finishing a cup of
    green tea
Far away, has landed

Sherrie's cancer cells, have bore through
The tunnel of the years, carrying Sherrie's youth
Passing through a long and pitch black tunnel

Sherrie, is in herself far away
UNI Air's birds land at Kinmen Shang Yi Airport
But, Sherrie's soul, is unable to land

Dad, carries your good friend, the camera
Sherrie, have you arrived at the airport yet
Let's take some photos together then

A Poem

Carrying, Sherrie's camera

Click, praising your kindness

Click, honoring your bravery

Blue sky, white clouds, a clear sky

Sherrie's lungs, prevail over tribulations

Walking through the tunnels, ascending to heaven

Wind Lion God, please tell me

How does one quash

The northeast wind's sorrow

Memory of memories, Tamsui

Facing Jiangong isle, taking photos

Composing the aura of sorrow

She is in heaven

I am in Kinmen

The sorrow of sunset

Open the camera lens, the waves of the ocean tell

That Sherrie is waving from the shore

The lens cannot focus

Sherrie is a Dot

A dot is everything

Sherrie

Is a dot's everything

A spot in life

A spot amongst ten thousand particles

Measures the infiniteness of the universe

Has Sherrie's dot withered

An astronomical number of spots

Weave a gigantic yet void spider

Captures in a net, the ablation of self

The dots of others and the limitlessness of the universe

Everything is the limitlessness of dots

Dots, Sherrie, everything is limitless

Note:Some sentences in the poem are copied from page 44 to page 45 of The Autobiography of Yayoi Kusama, Ecus Publishing House. After my daughter ascended to heaven, the dots of yearning covered my entire body, even the things she left behind had dots bespeckled over them.

How Many Centimeters

Life and death

Is only time conquering time.

-- Ye Di

To use a ruler to measure

Sherrie's whole life

How many centimeters of scenery would there be

On the ruler that measures

Birth and death

Are the graduation marks visible

I Weep

The night is deep, lay down

Stretching a bit, my hands, and feet

Bending a bit, my hands, and feet

My eyes attempt to open the window of dreams

Sherrie's lung adenocarcinoma

Surround the lungs, in a sit-in protest

I turn over, and bump into the wall

I turn back, and hit the wall

I weep only I can weep

My eyes silently remembering love

Not Cold at All

Sherrie

Lies in a freezer

It must be ice cold

Don't be afraid

Dad, Mom and Older Sister love your heart

We are keeping guard beside you, do not cry

Should you not find clothes to wear

Remember to quickly clothe our love

Upon your body, don't be shy

Dad, you don't need to worry

With you, Mom and Older Sister's love for me

Clothed upon my body, I am not cold at all

Dad, I Love You

I have been living in heaven for a year already
My days pass by in a very spring-like way

Grandma, Grandpa and Granddad all treat me very well
We often gather together to have dinner and to chat

Me, when I am free I will continue to take photos too
Dad, don't keep on losing the cameras

When I miss my family, I secretly fly down to the world
To sneak a look at how you all are doing, hee-hee……

Dad, there is no need to worry
I won't be a picky eater anymore

Dad, don't be sad
I can still receive calls on my cell phone

Don't Miss Me Anymore

Dad

Don't keep on missing, weeping

I'm sorry

I cannot let you hold my hand

And walk to that end of the carpet

Perhaps if I were to have a load of children

Whether they be boys or girls

Just like Grandpa holding Older Sister and my hands to take us to school

Don't keep on missing me

Dad, I'm in heaven

I'm not a picky eater anymore

And I'll develop the good habit of exercising

And I'll continue to take photos and continue to travel

And I'll... ...

And I'll miss weeping

Before and After

It's not a surprise that death appears via cancer
Only because "living" on earth is too lonely

-- Ye Di

Before getting sick
Everything was hope
Everything was dreams
Sitting down to chat, even the wind would make practical jokes

After getting sick
Praying to God
Pleading for help from Buddha
Pleading for help from the Ruler of Heaven
Pleading for help from doctors
Pleading for help from Death
Praying to dreams for hope
Imploring miracles from poetry

Purchasing time from the morning sun

Begging food to keep you alive

Kneeling in front of tomorrow to pray

Challenging one's own will

After death

The great ocean's everything returns to zero

The ebb tide waves' speaking voice can't be heard

The Sparrow That Flew Away

Reasons to keep on living
Are fewer and fewer

Reading, so many literary authors' works
Reading, so many philosophers' thoughts
Reading, so many artists' paintings
Yet, the lantern of hope is not to be found
Darkness always tells me, oh give up

I see a sparrow, solitarily staying on a branch
Jumping up and jumping down, looking and looking again
Arrows, normally fly towards the faraway distance

Reasons to keep on living
Become more and more obscure

Sherrie is like the sparrow on the branch

Arrows, normally fly towards the faraway distance

Reading Buddhist scripture, Buddha, is too a sparrow that has flown
away

Reading the Bible, Jesus, is too a sparrow that has flown away

And still cannot find a tree branch to perch and rest

Qingming Festival

We agreed, to live together

To often remember each other, in the Lord

We agreed, that there will be a day in the future

Where we will gather joyfully once more, in the Lord

Suddenly, a loud noise arises

It vomits out, sadness

It spits out, hurt

Reminiscing over the days past

There was laughter, and tears too

I am reluctant to tell you

In the love of the Lord, I am waiting for you

Days, stretch out their arms

They try to, wrap up

Sherrie's youth

I bless you in the Lord

I miss you in the Lord

May the Lord guide you

Into the land of Canaan

We agreed, not far

Simply, could not inhale

Her youth

We agreed, in the Lord

To hear, a turtledove on the roof

Gulu gululu

The sky, has brightened

Dew on the Hidden Orchid

Just like
A storage locker at the train station
Placed inside a small urn

Place her twenty-nine years of youth inside
No grassy meadows, to accompany
No cover of dense pines, to escort

The sun has a high fever
No fan, to blow
No air conditioner, to cool down

Sherrie, who cried without making a sound
The black night, reading
Li He's poem "The Tomb of Little Su"

When the gates of the underworld open

Remember to return home

To have a MOS Burger

Tamsui Station

UNI Air's solitary bird
From Kinmen Shang Yi Airport
Flying to Taipei Songshan Airport
(Dad has completed Sherrie's Kinmen trip)

We stayed at the Prelude to a Water Melody Family Inn
After dinner, Dad and Teacher Lin
Drank Kinmen Kaoliang 58 Liquor together, and talked about
Sherrie's passion for learning photography

Waking up in the morning, everyone, with cameras on our backs
Snapped shots, of the hoopoe bird's daily habitat
As always, Dad had trouble properly pressing the shutter
Rays of light, like to hide in dark places
I call out your nickname in a small voice, A-ying

Everyone, clicking, clicking, one after another

(Physical images cannot restore the truth)

The shutter is Dad's frame of mind

The ISO is the cell proliferation of the lung adenocarcinoma

The aperture is Sherrie's youth

In an unguarded moment, I yearn

The standard lens, rolls on the ground, it echoes

The camera falls to the ground, it echoes, yearning

(Sherrie would definitely say: "Dad, you stink! How clumsy of you!")

Sitting on the airplane

Outside the window, float snow-white fluffy clouds

Subtlety displaying, your sweet smile

UNI Air's solitary bird

Lands at Songshan Airport

Leaving Kinmen's tunnel of the years

Taking the Mass Rapid Transit, searching for Sherrie's bag

The eye-catching "Tamsui Line"

Is like a fruit knife

Peeling the skin off an apple

Peeling off, loneliness

Life lacks a bit of comfort from family

Sitting in a High Speed Rail train

My frame of mind mourns at high speed

Printing out Sherrie's history of pain and suffering

I ask the train conductor

Is Sherrie's train there

My Oldness

Sherrie, 29 years of age

Not yet old

And her life ended

Leaving behind, my oldness

Counting, longing

Legend

Lily flower, this is how it withered
Lung cancer seized upon, Sherrie's lungs

Lily flower, this is how it withered
Sherrie, struggled to free herself from Death's embrace

Lily flower, this is how it withered
Sherrie, could not take her camera away with her

Lily flower, this is how it withered
Sherrie, left behind the glistening of the stars

Lily flower, this is how it withered
Sherrie, withered   forever   withered

God, continue to allow people to pray
Buddha, continue to allow people to worship

Sherrie, left behind a legend in the world

The earth then continues to

Perhaps

And that the heavy sphere of Planet Earth
Will underneath our feet no more be turning

-- Marina Tsvetaeva

Sherrie who has disappeared from the world
The earth, cannot feel
A falling young leaf

One day
I too shall disappear from the world
Who knows who will still, carry on
Missing, her gentle name

Older Sister and her children
Perhaps will
After that who will …...

A Lifetime

There was not enough time for Sherrie

To reminisce upon   Dad

Yet had to   let Dad be bitterly hurt

Missing you   for a lifetime

Wipe Away

Sorrowful eyes

Are hard to wipe away

Hard to wipe away

Sherrie's lung adenocarcinoma

Weeping expressions in one's eyes

Are hard to wipe away

Hard to wipe away

Sherrie's lung adenocarcinoma

The eyes from dreams

Are hard to wipe away

Hard to wipe away

Sherrie's lung adenocarcinoma

The eyes of daybreak

Are hard to wipe away

Hard to wipe away

Sherrie's lung adenocarcinoma

The eyes of death

Can perhaps wipe away

Sherrie's lung adenocarcinoma

And let everything return to zero

The Moment Before Ascending to Heaven

The heart strives with every effort to free itself from
Death's black hands

The bed, trembles
Death's black hands

The doctor hides in the corner
And sighs

The sound of Sherrie's breathing
Alerts the earth
Awakens the heavens

The Blue-tailed Bee-eater

Fluttering my wings fulfilling a father's responsibility
An adventure with the courage to fly
To bite into a honeybee, how fat and juicy
Flying into the nest, releasing a father's loving kindness
The wings rouse the sound of joy
Feeding, my little treasure

After dinner, fluttering its wings soaring high beneath the moonlight
Hunting for delicious, delectable insects

The blue-tailed bee-eater, braving the big sun above
Performs aerial stunts, trapping honeybees

Sitting in the shade under the tree, stretching out a long lens
Searching for a trace of Sherrie
Dad too is a blue-tailed bee-eater that has lost its way
That cannot find the skies of blueness and white clouds

Sherrie, do you know

Dad too is a blue-tailed bee-eater

Sherrie, Sorry

Dad is not God, to rescue you, I cannot

Dad is not Buddha, to save you, I cannot

Dad is not Mazu, to bless and protect you, I cannot

Dad is not a doctor, to cure you, I cannot

Dad is only Dad… …

Dad can only weep

Dad can only hope

Dad very much wants to suffer on your behalf

Helpless

Dad nevertheless secretly weeps

Sherrie, you have now ascended to heaven

Dad still weeps… …

A Guppy

A bed enclosed with a mosquito net
A mosquito worms itself into the lungs and the cancer cells
Attacking together the lung bullae

In the small hours, the sound of Sherrie coughing
As punctual as an alarm clock, ringing
My wife and I, simultaneously without prior arrangement, stand
By her side driving away, Death

To live is to in fact be, roasted
Sherrie's pitch-black, future
The mischievous appearance from childhood, invades

"Dad, you must find for me a neurologist"
"Dad, I'm scared I'll become slow-witted!"
"Dad, hurry up and save me! … …"

Waking up, I am merely

A guppy trapped inside a fish tank

Sweet Young Leaf

Sherrie, a sweet young leaf

Dad overturns layer upon layer of leaves

Calling out to, the tree root's familial affection

I always believed you were very independent

Until you fell ill

Open the window where the heart is placed

You don't understand how to take care of your body

You don't take care of your body

Dad didn't get a chance, to tell you

I love you

Like a rose that withers early

Its petals, did not yet get a chance to be beautiful

Or even to sting

X-rays, Could Not Capture

X-rays, could not capture

The self-despair

About an illusory eternity, engraved

On a hard tortoiseshell

Reluctant for time to elapse through the days and nights

Eternity has been pickled by illness

Youth cannot find an exit

A winged steed, a rallying cry, galloping

Where did Sherrie's cancer cells originate from

Without finding a place to rest

Perhaps it was only a herd of wild beasts

That broke through the fences of the lungs

The night sky of the lungs, is covered with

Iressa, Doflex, Docetaxel ... ...

An array of stars is never to be found

Cancer cells have covered the night sky

X-rays, could not capture

God's halo

Where does God come from

Does He come from the sound of prayer

Oneself, in despair

Can sunlight penetrate inside

Today is itself eternity

A single wild lily at the bottom of the heart, swaying

A Visit to the Lung Lobes

I knock and knock, on the lung lobes' front door
"I am Sherrie's dad
Please allow me to enter
I would like to have a chat with the cancer cells' little angels"

"Go away!"
The lung lobes angrily say

"They are at battle in this very moment
The little angels became angry
They unceasingly impinge on the land of the white blood cells
The fighting is fierce
You cannot enter!"

I knock and knock, on the lung lobes' front door
"I am Sherrie's dad
Please allow me to enter

I would like to be a messenger of peace for the white blood cells
To persuade the little angels"

The lung lobes coldly reply
"Only Sherrie can persuade the little angels"

"The little angels only obey
Sherrie's confidence and perseverance
You, as a father
Pray!"

I knock and knock, on the lung lobes' front door
"I am Sherrie's dad
Please allow me to enter
My frame of mind must enter"

"Sherrie's lung lobes

Do not know Sherrie's dad

They don't even know Sherrie"

The lung lobes say, coolly

"There are no doors!"

Black Eyes

I had no courage to open

The black eyes that were given to me by the dark night

I carefully search among the photographs

For Sherrie's days of youth

There is a ray of light, which breaks through

The Bodhi tree, a living

Bright mirror-stand, reflecting light everywhere

The pain, Huineng you were wrong

Where can a bright mirror-stand be found, oh to no avail

To no avail can the bright mirror be made clean

The year 2016, it is known today

How to overturn, tomorrow

Tomorrow is a Bodhi tree

Each and every leaf

Are all bright mirror-stands

Yet in 2006

She was at Newcastle University in England

Chasing dreams

Before being able to see the bright mirror-stand

The Bodhi tree dried up

The black eyes that were given to me by the dark night

Could not find

The light lost by the day

Dreams, like shattered glass on the ground

No longer can it hold water, go ahead and insert a red rose!

A poem, like a cut of scarlet-red pork

Hanging in the sky

Crying out

Forget it

Me, in the valley of death

I straighten up my back, the plum flower blossoms once more

Name

Walking into the department store
I call out her name
Each and every young girl
Hides her name
Memories of yearning in the faraway heavens
It is impossible that I forget your name

Turning on the camera to take photos
There is always the sight of someone's back
Camera in hand, eye gazing through the viewfinder
A clicking sound, I can't tell if it is her or if it is me
It is impossible that I forget your name

I walk into your room
I open the drawer
I open the closet

I browse through the books in the bookcase

Ah! The name is covered in dust

Epilogue:Because people experience sadness, joy often slips away from
right beside us, immersed in sad times, mirrors have lost their
brightness, as if memories have wings. After completing the
writing of these poems, I don't know how to cherish the
time spent together, I always thought she would live longer
than me, this leaves me momentarily not knowing how to be
sorrowful.

Epilogy

I give thanks to my daughter Sherrie for letting Dad discover the true
face of death! Death is real!

> *Where that garden flows out*
> *and upends. It's in the living eyes*
> *of the lemon of the night:*
> *One blink is the dream,*
> *another is death singing*
> *now so silkily.*
> *And its cadenced voice is a young*
> *mother's whisper.*

-- Coral Bracho

Amended on December 27th, 2016

About the Author

Tsai Jung-yung (b. 1955) is currently an editing member of *Li Poetry Society*, a director in *Taiwan Modern Poets'Association*, a director and editing member of the children's literature magazine *"Serissa Fetida"*, and a member of *PPDM*. He participated International Poetry Festivals held respectively in Mongolia, Cuba and Chile.

About the Translators

Jane Deasy is an Irish-born, Taiwan-raised, Vancouver-based Mandarin Chinese Translator and Interpreter. She is an Associate Member of The Society of Translators and Interpreters of British Columbia and a Member of the Literary Translators' Association of Canada (Concordia University, Montreal) .

CONTENTS

語言文學類　PG1982　台灣詩叢06

念念詩穎 Continuous Thoughts of Sherrie
——蔡榮勇漢英雙語詩集

作　　者/蔡榮勇（Tsai Jung-yung）
譯　　者/戴珍妮（Jane Deasy）
叢書策劃/李魁賢（Lee Kuei-shien）
責任編輯/林昕平
圖文排版/周妤靜
封面設計/蔡瑋筠

發 行 人/宋政坤
法律顧問/毛國樑　律師
出版發行/秀威資訊科技股份有限公司
　　　　　114台北市內湖區瑞光路76巷65號1樓
　　　　　電話：+886-2-2796-3638　傳真：+886-2-2796-1377
　　　　　http://www.showwe.com.tw
劃撥帳號/19563868　戶名：秀威資訊科技股份有限公司
　　　　　讀者服務信箱：service@showwe.com.tw
展售門市/國家書店（松江門市）
　　　　　104台北市中山區松江路209號1樓
　　　　　電話：+886-2-2518-0207　傳真：+886-2-2518-0778
網路訂購/秀威網路書店：http://store.showwe.tw
　　　　　國家網路書店：http://www.govbooks.com.tw

2018年2月　BOD一版
定價：200元
版權所有　翻印必究
本書如有缺頁、破損或裝訂錯誤，請寄回更換

國家圖書館出版品預行編目

念念詩穎 Continuous Thoughts of Sherrie：蔡榮
勇漢英雙語詩集 / 蔡榮勇著；戴珍妮譯. -- 一
版. -- 臺北市：秀威資訊科技, 2018.02
　　面；　公分. -- (台灣詩叢；6)
BOD版
ISBN 978-986-326-524-5(平裝)

851.486   107000448

讀 者 回 函 卡

感謝您購買本書，為提升服務品質，請填妥以下資料，將讀者回函卡直接寄回或傳真本公司，收到您的寶貴意見後，我們會收藏記錄及檢討，謝謝！如您需要了解本公司最新出版書目、購書優惠或企劃活動，歡迎您上網查詢或下載相關資料：http:// www.showwe.com.tw

您購買的書名：＿＿＿＿＿＿＿＿＿＿＿＿＿＿＿＿＿＿＿＿＿＿＿

出生日期：＿＿＿＿＿年＿＿＿＿＿月＿＿＿＿日

學歷：□高中 (含) 以下　　□大專　　□研究所 (含) 以上

職業：□製造業　□金融業　□資訊業　□軍警　□傳播業　□自由業
　　　□服務業　□公務員　□教職　　□學生　□家管　□其它＿＿＿＿

購書地點：□網路書店　□實體書店　□書展　□郵購　□贈閱　□其他

您從何得知本書的消息？

　　□網路書店　□實體書店　□網路搜尋　□電子報　□書訊　□雜誌

　　□傳播媒體　□親友推薦　□網站推薦　□部落格　□其他＿＿＿＿＿

您對本書的評價：(請填代號　1.非常滿意　2.滿意　3.尚可　4.再改進)

　　封面設計＿＿＿　版面編排＿＿＿　內容＿＿＿　文／譯筆＿＿＿　價格＿＿＿

讀完書後您覺得：

　　□很有收穫　□有收穫　□收穫不多　□沒收穫

對我們的建議：＿＿＿＿＿＿＿＿＿＿＿＿＿＿＿＿＿＿＿＿＿＿＿

＿＿＿＿＿＿＿＿＿＿＿＿＿＿＿＿＿＿＿＿＿＿＿＿＿＿＿＿＿＿＿

＿＿＿＿＿＿＿＿＿＿＿＿＿＿＿＿＿＿＿＿＿＿＿＿＿＿＿＿＿＿＿

＿＿＿＿＿＿＿＿＿＿＿＿＿＿＿＿＿＿＿＿＿＿＿＿＿＿＿＿＿＿＿

11466
台北市內湖區瑞光路 76 巷 65 號 1 樓

秀威資訊科技股份有限公司　　　收

BOD 數位出版事業部

....

（請沿線對折寄回，謝謝！）

姓　　名：＿＿＿＿＿＿＿＿＿　年齡：＿＿＿＿　性別：□女　□男

郵遞區號：□□□□□

地　　址：＿＿＿＿＿＿＿＿＿＿＿＿＿＿＿＿＿＿＿＿＿

聯絡電話：(日)＿＿＿＿＿＿＿＿＿　(夜)＿＿＿＿＿＿＿＿＿

E-mail：＿＿＿＿＿＿＿＿＿＿＿＿＿＿＿＿＿＿＿＿＿